for Bryan and Jeremy S.C.
for Joe and Ellen J.B.

Text copyright © Susan Cooper 2002
Illustrations copyright © Jane Browne 2002

The rights of Susan Cooper and Jane Browne to be identified as the author and illustrator of this work have been asserted
by them in accordance with the Copyright, Designs and Patents Act, 1988.

First published in the United Kingdom 2002 by
The Bodley Head Children's Books,
Random House, 20 Vauxhall Bridge Road, London SW1V 2SA

Random House Australia (Pty) Limited
20 Alfred Street, Milsons Point, Sydney
New South Wales 2061, Australia

Random House New Zealand Limited
18 Poland Road, Glenfield
Auckland 10, New Zealand

Random House South Africa (Pty) Limited
Endulini, 5a Jubilee Road,
Parktown 2193, South Africa

THE RANDOM HOUSE GROUP Limited Reg. No. 954009
www.randomhouse.co.uk

Papers used by Random House are natural, recyclable products made from
wood grown in sustainable forests. The manufacturing processes conform
to the environmental regulations of the country of origin.

A CIP catalogue record for this book is available from the British Library.

ISBN 0-370-32635-0

Printed in Singapore

Frog

Susan Cooper
Illustrated by Jane Browne

THE BODLEY HEAD
LONDON

Little Joe couldn't swim.

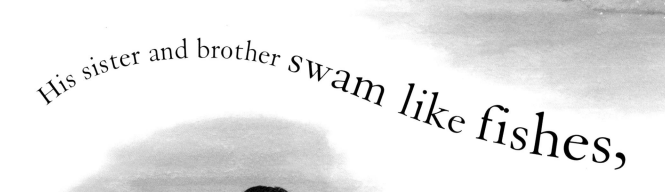

His sister and brother swam like fishes,

his mum s w a m like a submarine.

But Little Joe just didn't get it.
He splashed about

— and everyone laughed.

Little Joe was sad.

That day a frog came hopping
towards the swimming pool; a very
small frog, from a pond not far away.
He hopped into the pool
and swam, kicking with his
strong back legs.

Little Joe watched, and smiled.

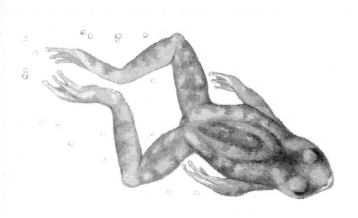

The pool was much deeper
than Frog's pond,
and the sides weren't soft and muddy,
but hard and slippery.
Frog bumped his head.

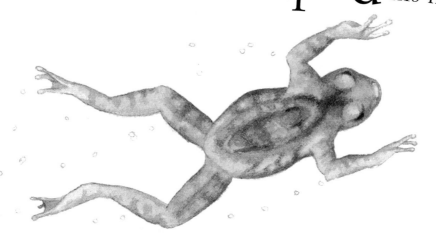

He swam to and fro,

trying to get out,

but he couldn't jump over the edge,

and he couldn't climb up the sides.

Frog was scared.

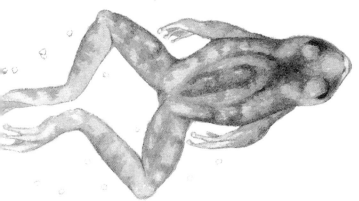

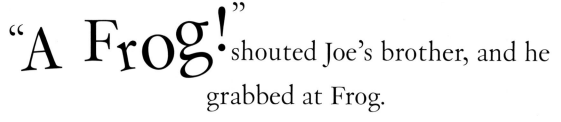

"A Frog!" shouted Joe's brother, and he
grabbed at Frog.

Frog just managed to dodge away.

"Gross!" screamed Joe's sister, and she splashed at Frog.

Frog swam down to the bottom of the pool,
very fast. Joe's Dad came with a net and
tried to scoop Frog into it;

Joe's Mum tried to chase him into the net.
They all splashed about like
lunatics, trying to catch Frog.

Soon Joe's family got bored with their frog
chase, so they stopped for lemonade.
Frog kicked himself up from the bottom
of the pool to the edge, near Joe.

He was very tired, and
very, very scared.

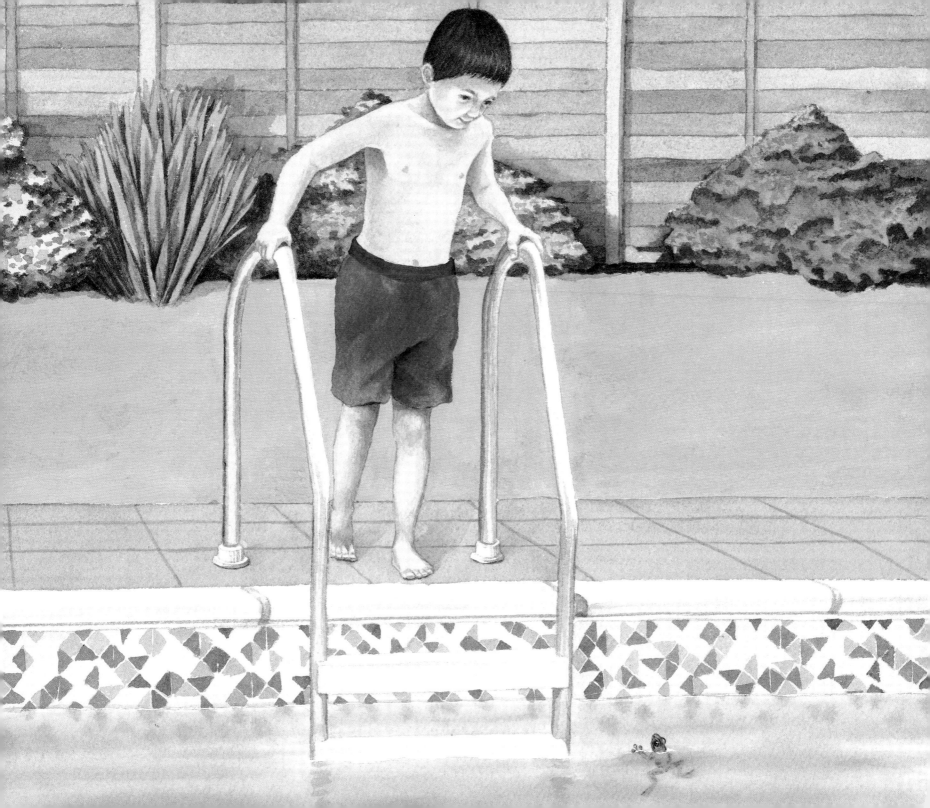

Little Joe got into the pool.
He moved slowly, slowly towards
Frog, and put out his hand.
Very carefully he moved his hand up
under Frog's feet until Frog was
sitting on his palm, and he lifted
Frog very gently out
of the water.

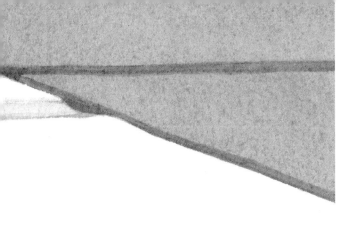

Frog and Little Joe looked at each other.

Joe whispered,

"Go home, Frog.

Go home where it's safe."

Frog looked back at Little Joe.

With his strong back legs Frog **hopped** away, over the grass, under the fence, back to his pond.

Little Joe watched him go.

Then he looked at the water.
He took a deep breath,
and he **kicked** with his legs,

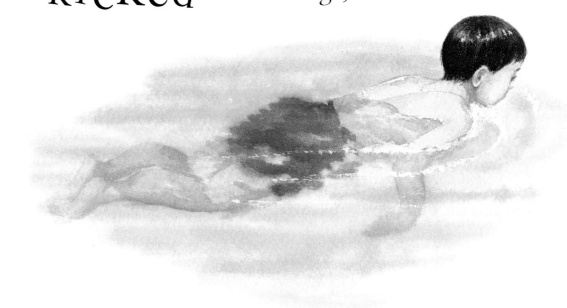

...across the pool

and he swam all the way ...

... just like Frog.